This Orchard book
belongs to

_____

_____

_____

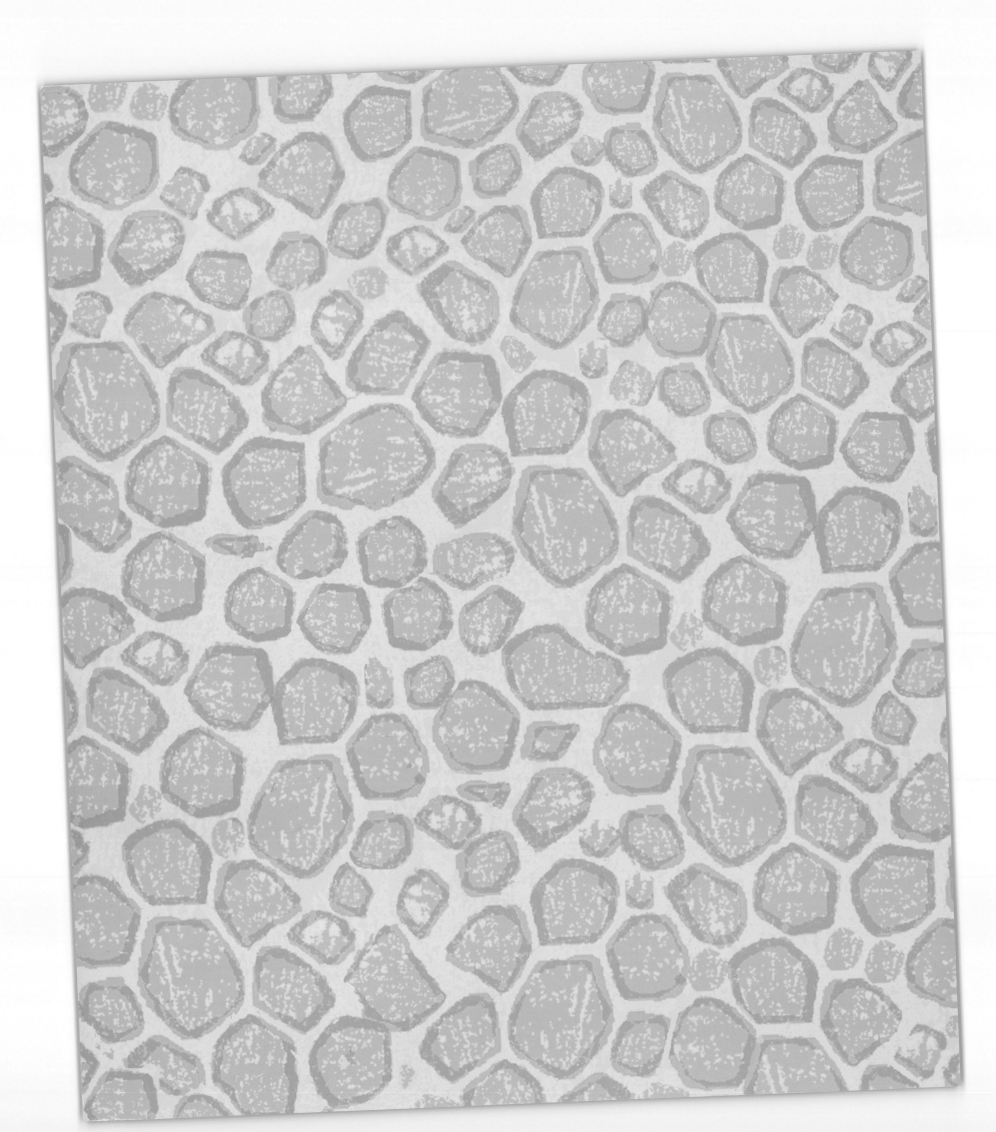

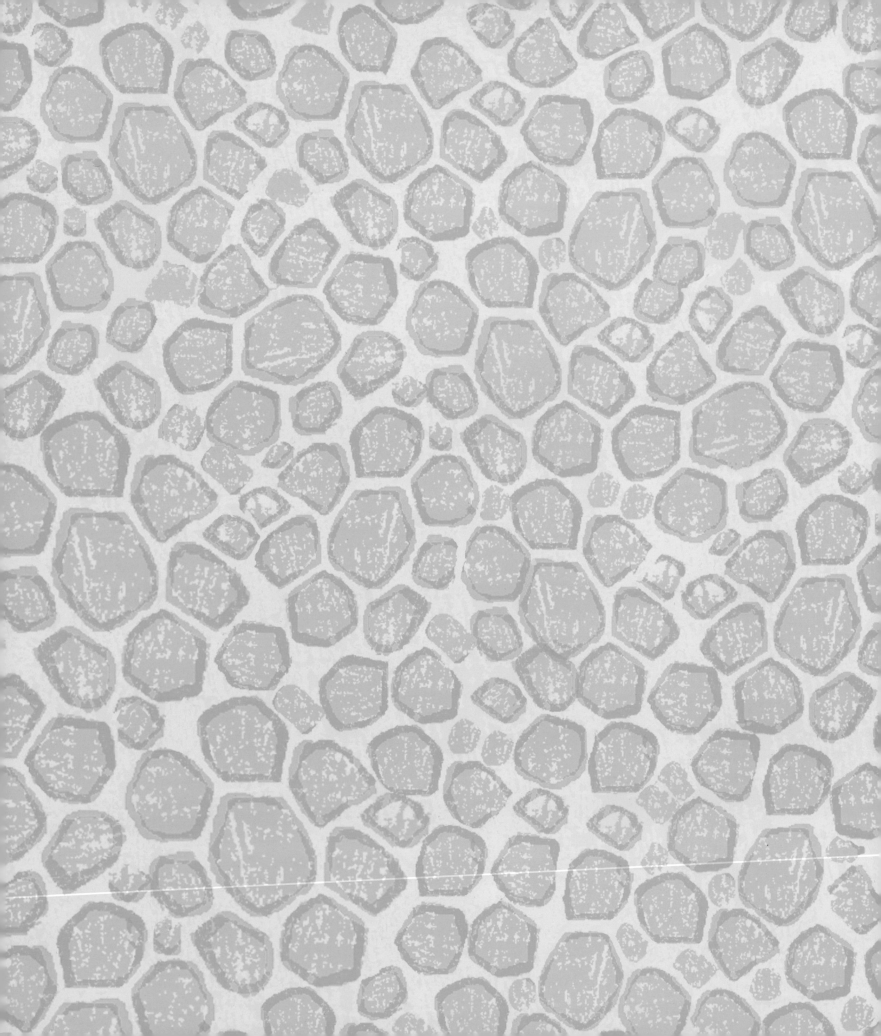

For Will,
with love, Giles

For Paula,
with love, Emma

ORCHARD BOOKS

First published in Great Britain in 2017 by The Watts Publishing Group
This edition first published in 2018

1 3 5 7 9 10 8 6 4 2

Text © Giles Andreae 2017
Illustrations © Emma Dodd 2017

The moral rights of the author and illustrator have been asserted.

A CIP catalogue record for this book is available from the British Library.

ISBN 978 1 40834 557 3

Printed and bound in China

Orchard Books
An imprint of Hachette Children's Group
Part of The Watts Publishing Group Limited
Carmelite House, 50 Victoria Embankment, London EC4Y 0DZ

An Hachette UK Company
www.hachette.co.uk
www.hachettechildrens.co.uk

I love my dinosaur

Giles Andreae & Emma Dodd

ORCHARD

I love my friendly dinosaur!

He sleeps here on my bedroom floor.

It keeps him feeling safe, you see,

To know he's curled

up next to me.

It's morning. Yippee! Breakfast time.

His bowl is HUGE. Now look at mine!

We like to clean our teeth together.

I help him, as his take FOREVER.

And now it's time
to go to school.
His scooter's looking
very cool!

My dinosaur likes painting best,

Which makes our teacher get quite stressed.

At break time, we love playing games

And swinging on the climbing frames.

At home, he likes to help us cook. He makes some pretty weird stuff – LOOK!

It's bedtime now, so jim-jams on,

While Daddy sings

us both a song.

"It's sleepy time," we hear him say,

"Tomorrow is another day.

"So tuck away those

little claws . . .

Sweet dreams, my darling dinosaurs!"

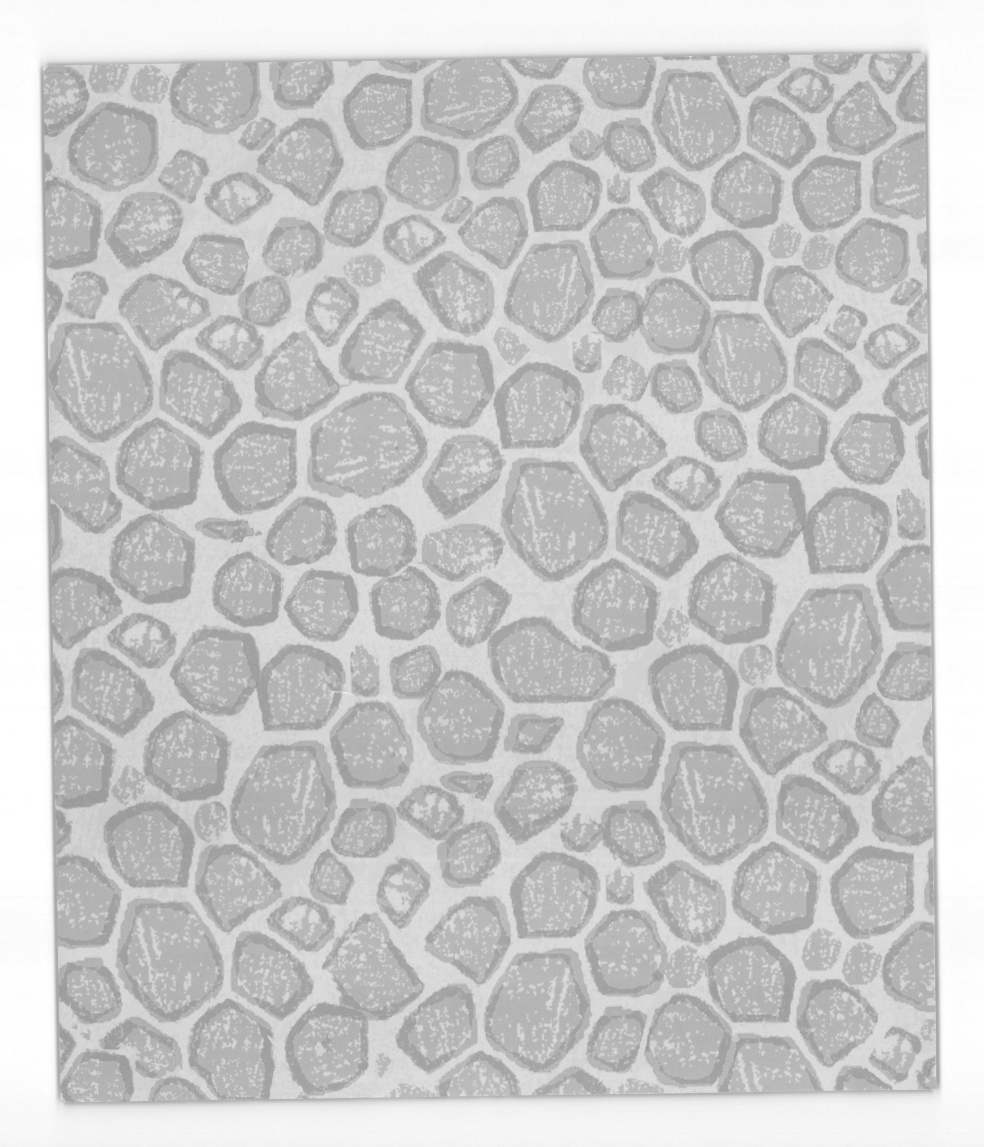

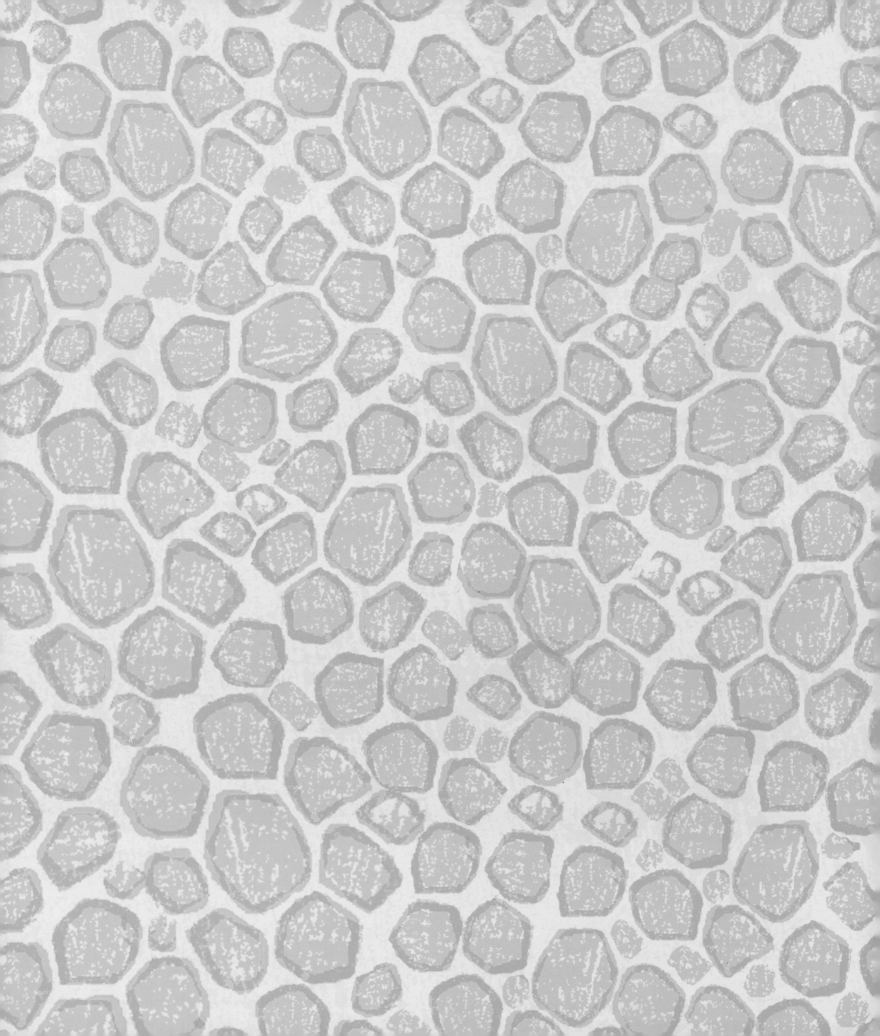